WHERE POPPIES GROW

A WORLD WAR I COMPANION

Linda Granfield

Fitzhenry & Whiteside

First published in 2001 by Stoddart Kids
Published in Canada in 2002 by Fitzhenry & Whiteside, 195 Allstate Parkway, Markham,
Ontario L3R 4T8
Published in the United States in 2002 by Fitzhenry & Whiteside, 121 Harvard Avenue,
Suite 2, Allston, Massachusetts 02134

www.fitzhenry.ca   godwit@fitzhenry.ca

Canada Cataloguing in Publication Data

Granfield, Linda

Where poppies grow: a World War I companion

Includes index
ISBN 0-7737-3319-1

1. World War, 1914-1918 – Juvenile literature. I Title.

D522.7.G73 2001   j940.3   C2001-900889-9

*An anecdotal overview of World War I illustrating how ordinary lives were changed by global-scale conflict, and
humanizing the sacrifice made by so many.*

*We acknowledge for their financial support of our publishing program the Canada Council, the Ontario Arts
Council, and the Government of Canada through the Book Publishing Industry Development Program (BPIDP).*

Printed and bound in Canada

for Fred Heather

in honor of his 90th year

Per Ardua Ad Astra

*Note: Passages printed in italics are actual words taken from the
back of the image or a contemporary document.*

She cradles a new baby in a starched christening gown. A fresh rose is pinned at her breast. A locket with her husband's photograph hangs from her neck. She tentatively looks at the camera. This unnamed family's life is about to change . . .

WAR!!!

When the First World War, the Great War, began in August 1914, no one knew that millions of young men and women would die before the conflict ended in 1918. No one knew that villages would be erased from the map, or that entire nations would be changed forever. In fact, people thought the war would be over before Christmas.

There was no single reason why the war began. Some European countries, like Germany, craved more power. Others, like France, wanted revenge for past wrongs, while Britain feared Germany's growing fleet and industrial power. People were primed for war. The murder of the heir to the Austro-Hungarian throne, in June 1914, was the spark that lit this ready tinder.

A Grade Eight graduation photo, Canada, 1914. Dressed in their finest clothes, these youths look to the future. For many, the picture records their final day as students. Some will continue their education. War, however, will be declared before the summer closes. For some of these boys, there will be no class reunion. They will enlist and never return.

The back reads: *How do you like this toffee soldier? . . . He swanks about being in the army four days.* How old is he, this young man willing to go to war? A soldier was supposed to be at least eighteen years old. Sadly, many younger boys lied about their age and were accepted.

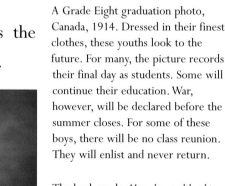

A photo of my brother George, writes Frank A. Jefferis. In many families, older brothers enlisted soon after war was declared. Younger brothers followed as the years passed and the Canadian and British Expeditionary Forces needed more soldiers. By 1917, young volunteers were in short supply. The Military Service Act was passed in Canada and men were conscripted, or forced to enlist.

When the German army moved into neutral Belgium, Britain upheld its treaty obligations to defend the Belgians. On August 4, 1914, the British government announced: "War, Germany, act." Britain, joined by other supportive countries called "Allies," was at war!

But the Great War was unlike any other in history. It was a new and horrible artillery battle fought from rat-infested, water-filled trenches dug deep into foreign soil. The only noble thing about it was the dedication of the millions who fought for what they believed.

Into the nightmarish terrain of the Western Front stepped thousands of soldiers from many countries. As you gaze upon the faces of some of these people, pause for a moment and consider who they were. Linger on their heart-felt words written home. How many of them returned to their families? Their faces are our faces, their deeds our inheritance.

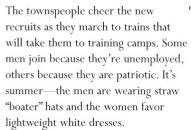

MISS VESTA TILLEY IN KHAKI

The proceeds of the sale of these cards will be handed by Miss TILLEY to one of the War Relief Funds

The colorful British vaudeville star with the stage name Vesta Tilley (born Matilda Alice Powles) was a male impersonator. During the war, she helped recruit men for the armed forces. She appeared in uniform, sang rousing military songs and was called "England's Greatest Recruiting Sergeant." She sold postcards like this one to raise War Relief Funds.

The townspeople cheer the new recruits as they march to trains that will take them to training camps. Some men join because they're unemployed, others because they are patriotic. It's summer—the men are wearing straw "boater" hats and the women favor lightweight white dresses.

5

Kits and Kilts

New recruits had lots to learn during their training period at camps like the one in Valcartier, Quebec. There they found acres of tents, thousands of horses, and piles of khaki uniforms. It was time to stop being a farmer, a banker, or a businessman and become a soldier.

(above) Many young men had professional photographs taken to send home to their loved ones. These posed photos usually show the military uniforms and equipment at their best, before they became muddied and worn out at the Front. This portrait shows the shiny boots and buttons, the swagger-stick (short cane) and the puttees (strips of fabric) that were wrapped tightly around the socks and pantlegs.

(right) The Morning Wash in a Canadian camp. No porcelain sinks and velour towels — just rough wooden trestle tables, cracked enamel basins, and raggedy linens.

WITH THE CANADIANS IN THEIR ENGLISH CAMP.
"SCOTTIES" FROM OVERSEAS.   OFFICERS OF THE CANADIAN HIGHLANDERS.

(left) These Canadian Highlanders wear jackets with expandable pockets and khaki covers over their wool kilts. Spats cover the lower sock and upper boot. "Khaki" is a Hindu word that refers to the color of the cotton or wool fabric. It means "dust-colored" — useful camouflage when soldiers were on the battlefield or in the forests.

(above) Kit inspection. A soldier's kit included his clothing, blankets, and other gear he needed. (A soldier carried about 75 pounds (30 kilograms) of kit, ammunition, and weapons.) It was his job to keep his kit in good repair. This became increasingly difficult during the war years as items became hard to replace. Many kit items had more than one use: for instance, tin hats were used as shaving basins.

WALL SCALING—AN IMPORTANT PART OF INFANTRY TRAINING

(above) Physical fitness increased a soldier's ability to protect himself and his fellow infantrymen on the battlefield. These American soldiers (the United States joined the Allies against Germany in 1917) try their best to get over the wall.

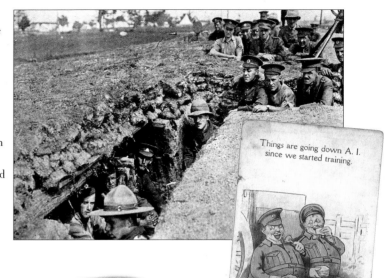

(right) Dig, dig, dig. *The object of the training of the body is to develop in the soldier a capacity for resisting fatigue and privation.* The practice trenches these recruits carved out of Canadian soil were an introduction to the water-logged pits in France that they would be calling home in the months and years to come.

Things are going down A. I. since we started training.

(above) Soldiers wrote home from the camps complaining about the noise, the crowding, and the boredom. They also sent home humorous cards like this one that poked fun at the amounts of food they were consuming. For those who had been unemployed before enlisting, the repetitious drilling at camp was a price they were willing to pay for meals and clothing.

56   CHAPTER II.   [Sec. 62.

through the barrel, the thumb-nail of the right hand being placed in front of the bolt to reflect light into the barrel.

The soldier, when the officer has passed the next file to him, will act as detailed in Sec. **60, 2**.

Notes.—i. If it is necessary to examine arms, the men, when in the position of *for inspection, port arms*, will be cautioned to remain at the *port*. Ranks will be closed, as in Sec. **60, 2**, when the examination has been completed.

ii. In ordering arms from the examine, the first motion is to seize the rifle with the right hand between the back-sight and the band, at the same time bringing the left foot back to the right. With the second motion the rifle will be brought to the order, the left hand being cut away to the side.

62. *To trail arms from the order, and vice versá* (Plate X).

1. Trail—Arms.

By a slight bend of the right arm give the rifle a cant forward and seize it at the point of balance, bringing it at *e* to a horizontal position at the side at the full extent of the right arm, which should hang easily from the shoulder, fingers and thumb round the rifle.

2. Order—Arms.

Raise the muzzle, catch the rifle at the band (with Lee-Enfield or Lee-Metford rifle at the lower band) and come to the *order*.

Note.—The *trail* is not to be used in close order drill except by rifle regiments.

It will be used when required for movements in the field in both close and extended order.

PLATE X.   *To face p. 56.*

(left) The "Infantry" was the body of soldiers who marched and fought on foot. The training manual is 250 pages long and filled with small print, teaching everything the soldier was expected to know and do. The book tells how to fight in a village or forest, how to fire a machine gun, and how to listen quietly for the enemy.

To England's Green Fields

After their training was completed, troops were sent to England. They shared ships with tons of equipment and supplies. Before they left, there might be some celebrations with their families, trips into the downtown taverns in big cities, and parades. Then it was off to the awaiting gangways, crowded ships, seasickness, and finally . . . England. *At long last,* they wrote, *we are almost on the battlefields of Europe.*

(above) A mother attends to her baby as troops, trained and anxious to leave, parade down University Avenue in Toronto. The Ontario Parliament Building looms on the horizon. (Famed actress Mary Pickford, who starred in silent films during the war years, was born in one of the row houses on the right.)

(below) A flotilla of tugboats assists a Canadian troop ship as it leaves for England. (The flag is "the Red Ensign," used as Canada's national flag until 1965.)

Once in England, there was more training, such as bayonet practice on Salisbury Plain. The training manual says: *The main essential to success in battle is to close with the enemy, cost what it may.* Canadian, British, and American troops in Flanders, as elsewhere in this World War, were taught *to produce such a high degree of courage and disregard of self, that in the stress of battle [they would] use [their] brains and weapons coolly and to the best advantage . . .*

Canadian Recruits undergo training at Salisbury.

Across the Channel to Flanders

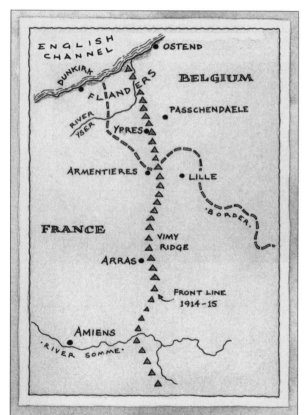

Many of the troops sent to Europe put their training to the test in Flanders, the French and Belgian lands bordered by the English Channel. For centuries, Flanders was the site of fertile farmlands and cities that were bustling mercantile centers trading with the world, and now it was the epicenter of the war. Troops arrived to find medieval guildhalls destroyed by bombardments, and fields stripped of topsoil and pockmarked by shell craters. In this horrific environment, the soldiers prepared to meet the enemy. Nearly half a million Allied soldiers lived and fought in the dreary trenches on the Western Front. There were three lines of trenches: the front line (closest to the enemy), the support line, and the reserve line. Men moved about between the three lines through communicating trenches, and through tunnels dug by men called "sappers."

(right) Trenches were at least six feet (two meters) deep and could be lined with sandbags or corrugated metal. At the far end of the trench is the firing step on which the soldiers stood to fire across "No Man's Land," the 300 feet (30 meters) of battlefield that separated them from the enemy's trenches. The wooden duckboards on the ground were meant to keep the men's feet out of the mud and could be used as portable ladders and bridges.

. . . and the Trenches

(right) The close conditions in trenches (here filled with Belgian soldiers) led to infestations of lice and the spread of disease. Snow and rain filled the trenches and had no place to go. Therefore, men often spent days standing in knee-high, filthy water. This led to a condition called "trench foot," where the skin rotted from the bone. Frostbite led to amputation. For a young man used to the open skies of the English fields or North American prairies, the confinements of the trenches could lead to severe claustrophobia.

(above) British soldiers (called "Tommies") sit in the "funk holes" of a German trench. Their unshaven faces illustrate that the rule *a soldier shall be clean-shaven at all times* has been ignored. In battle conditions, there was no time for personal hygiene. Only when a soldier was sent out of the trenches "to the rear," could he enjoy a hot bath and some decent food.

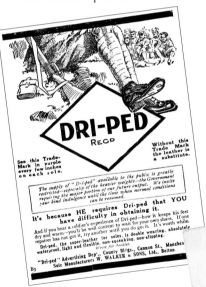

(above) A magazine advertisement for "Dri-Ped" claims it is *absolutely waterproof*. The illustration shows a soldier's puttee-wrapped legs and very dry feet. Letters sent home from the Front, however, told a different story.

I'm gonna' fight, but gee! I hope I don't get stuck in the trenches.

(left) Despite the horrible conditions, soldiers still found a way to laugh at being "stuck in the trenches."

(above) Branches stripped from nearby forests provide the wall supports in this trench. A British soldier looks over the top, or parapet. During the daylight hours, men waited and listened. Many complained of headaches because of the constant noise of gunfire and exploding shells. Some slept or played cards. Everyone listened to the groans of the injured, trapped on the field above. At night, supplies and food could be moved safely, out of the enemy's sight. In the darkness, troops repaired the trenches, carried out night raids, and tried to rescue the injured.

The Routine of Daily Life

When not in the trenches, a soldier had plenty to keep him busy. There were communication lines and trucks to repair. Horses had to be exercised. Laundry had to be collected — and lice (chats) had to be picked out of the seams of the supposedly clean garments. The routine of war was offset by the promise of time "on leave," time for fun and recuperation.

(above) Soldiers got their meals in different ways. If possible, some food was cooked and delivered to the trenches. Other meals were eaten in mess halls, or in the home kitchens of Flanders, or in an *estaminet* (canteen). Here, three cooks take a moment from their work. A row of ovens lines the left wall. The slippery water on the floor and the few small light fixtures must have made their tasks difficult.

(left) Fresh bread is baked at the field bakery and put onto trucks for delivery. The ovens are on the right. At the left, camp cookers heat the famous stew (see page 13). In the foreground, bread dough has been left to rise under white cloths.

A Field Bakery

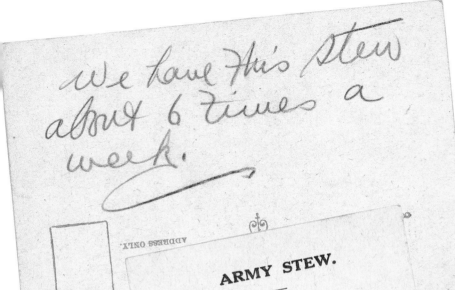

We have this stew about 6 times a week.

ADDRESS ONLY.

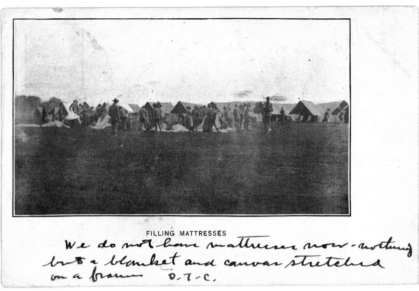

FILLING MATTRESSES

We do not have mattresses now — nothing but a blanket and canvas stretched on a frame. D.T.C.

Some of the tedious work done when not in battle. The picture shows men filling mattresses. The handwriting says *we do not have mattresses now — nothing but a blanket and canvas stretched on a frame.*

ARMY STEW.

You see in the papers every day
Pictures of Tommy at work and at play,
As healthy a chap as you'd wish to meet
And you wonder whatever they give him to eat.

I can't give you all, though the list is not long
Of the stuff that makes him so healthy and strong,
But the mixture I'm going to describe to you
Is that mystery of mysteries—Army Stew.

An Army dixie has first to be got,
Perhaps it's a clean one, perhaps it is not
It may contain tea-leaves from yesterdays tea
Such trifles the cook is not supposed to see.

Bully-beef cut into squares and some "Spuds"
Bacon Rind and sausages (perhaps "Duds"),
Lumps of fat, skin, gristle, bone and some Duff
All nicely browned with a dose of Cooks snuff.

Winkles, shrimps, kippers, one bean and a pea
Perhaps a few rissoles that are "Buckshee"
Some dripping and bread, porridge and baked rice
All go in with the sugar and spice.

Cabbage, suet, tomatoes and currie
Enter the dixie in a great hurry
To be stirred and boiled and stirred and when the
Stew is opened the boys begin to sing

OH! FOR A ROLEY POLEY MOTHER
USE TO MAKE!

Copyright

I.C., E.C.

This postcard pokes fun at the boring menu of bully-beef (canned corned beef), beans, and plum jam. A "dixie" is a cooking pot, "rissoles" are fried ground meat cakes, and "Buckshee" means free. A "roley poley" is an English dessert. On the back of the card (top) the sender speaks the truth. He, like thousands of other soldiers, wants some homecooking.

When a soldier, wounded or not, had a few days leave, he often went to a city, like London, for entertainment. This advertisement demonstrates how appreciative businessmen, often too old themselves to enlist, offered their defenders hospitality. *Walk, hop, crawl, or be carried in . . .*

In contrast, able-bodied young men who had not enlisted were often accosted on the streets by women who pinned white feathers, the sign of cowardice, to their lapels.

Over the Top

New technology meant new weaponry and more savage warfare in this war than had ever been seen before. Poor weather conditions from 1914 through 1918 made marches and battles long and exhausting. Numbed by the furious noise, knee-deep in mud, and facing death daily, many went mad.

Working party starting off, wearing waterproof sheets and trench-waders.

(above right) When troops were ordered to go "over the top" they scrambled up and over the edge of the trench and onto No Man's Land. Before they reached the German trenches they would have to maneuver over shell craters and through barbed wire, at the same time dodging machine-gun fire, a near-impossible task. Notice how much equipment each man is carrying on his back as he runs. If the fellow running next to you was hit, you were not to stop and look after him — you had to keep moving forward. Someone might return to the field later to find your comrade.

(above) The misery is best portrayed by a infantryman's own words: *The night of Friday, April 21st [1915], was dark and wet, and it had been pouring with rain for some time previously. The ground across which the attacking force . . . had to go was a quagmire of the worst kind. The mud was never less than knee-deep, and frequently it was up to the thighs. At times, the men could only advance by throwing their rifles forward and going after them like frogs. So bad was it that the front column [of men] took several hours to cover two hundred yards, a distance which a sprinter would run in twenty-five seconds. All the time, bullets were whizzing through the gloom, shells were bursting, and now and again machine guns got to work.*

(right) Belgian machine gunners take aim at the German trenches. This painting of the 1914 Battle of the Yser (a river in Flanders) shows the chaos of battle. The lower branches of the trees have been stripped for use as trench timber, firewood, even splints.

After battles were over, soldiers moved through the
fields looking for wounded allies that could be helped,
or enemy troops who would become prisoners of war. Items
that would be treated as souvenirs of war were also picked up from the battlefields. These
two scuffed photographs (above middle and right) are eerie reminders of this kind of memento-hunting.
On the back of the image of the young German soldier in his dirty, torn uniform is written: *Found on the*
Battlefield by Cpl. J. Bashaw, Aug 8 & 9 1918. The Battle of Amiens was fought August 8 to 11 that year.

The mother-and-sons photo
(above) also has Bashaw's handwriting on the
back: *This German gave me this card as he was about to Dye. Aug 9/18.*
Keep these . . . as a good Souvenir. Note the blood on the Corner.

It is sad to imagine the scene these photographs
bring to mind. As the British corporal walks across the
field, a German soldier, mortally wounded, calls to
him. In his bloodied hand he holds a picture of his
family. He waves it at the passing corporal. Did he ask
Bashaw to tell his family something? Could Bashaw
understand his German words? Like every other man
in that battle, the German soldier was a person with
loved ones who waited for his return. We can only
wonder what happened to his family.

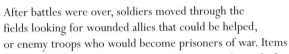

German Prisoners

(left) A stereoscope was a hand-held device that held a
card showing two photographs of the same object,
taken at slightly different angles. When viewed through
the stereoscope lens, the two images became one with
a three-dimensional effect. This World War I
stereoscope card features German prisoners of war
(with a splash of color for special "realistic quality").

On Flanders Fields

War remembrance memorials list the names of important First World War battles — names that during the war years were readily recognized by school children around the world: Mons, Ypres, Neuve Chapelle, the Somme, Beaumont Hamel, Vimy and Cambrai. Modern equipment brought a new destructive swiftness to these battles and a new element to war stories.

Before the days of wireless communications, line telegraphs and field telephones were the principal means of giving or receiving news on the Western Front. Cable lines had to be buried six feet (two meters) in the earth in order to protect them from shell blasts. During the rainy periods, it was difficult to maintain these lines in the mud.

A BROADSIDE FROM OUR LAND-SHIP.

Canadian Official

This puts the tin hat on it !!

Poison gas was an insidious new weapon used by both sides beginning in 1915. Some of the gas caused the lungs to fill up with fluid and the soldier "drowned." Mustard gas damaged the inside and outside of the body.

Dr. Cluny Macpherson of Newfoundland invented the gas helmet to provide protection. By the summer of 1916, the Small Box Respirator became standard issue and deaths from gas became relatively rare.

Cartoonists played with the odd appearances of the various models of gas masks. One such example (above) also gives a good look at a soldier's gear.

(above) Imagine the fear as the first tanks used in action rolled over the battlefields. A British magazine described them: *the tanks have the appearance of whales floating on the sea-surface as they crawled towards the German lines . . . The bullets pattering on our side sounded like peas or hailstones on the roof of a galvanized tin shed, and then, as we got nearer, like the blows of an erratic and jumpy pneumatic hammer.* The early tanks had difficulty moving over the rutted battlefields and were sometimes abandoned at the side of the road or in a mud-filled crater.

(left) The consequences of the new technology. This burial scene was repeated thousands of times during the war in Flanders. The nurse who owned this photograph wrote: *this is the simple funeral which takes place for the ordinary soldier. One officer, one non-commissioned officer, ten men and two buglers.* A chaplain reads the final prayers. A group of women, and a few distracted children, stand in the strong sunlight and pay their respects.

Warfare on the Seas. . .

Before the First World War, a trip by ocean liner was one of the most memorable ways to spend a vacation. People who could afford first-class tickets traveled in cabins decked in finery. Other passengers enjoyed fewer comforts, but lined up to buy tickets nevertheless.

During the war years, sea travel was curtailed because of the German submarines or U-boats ("U" represented "*ünter*" in German, "under" in English), that lurked beneath the Atlantic's waters. In 1915, the enemy torpedoed the liner RMS *Lusitania* and the ship sank in under thirty minutes. Over one thousand people (some of them Americans), perished. This act of aggression was a factor that later brought the United States into the war.

This December 1916 magazine cover highlights the power and drama of war at sea. The "Optimistic After-the-War Outlook" article mentioned on the cover is a bit premature, for the end of the war won't come for nearly another two years.

Passenger ships, like the RMS *Mauretania*, were pressed into military service during the war. Troops and supplies had to be delivered from North America to England and then on to Europe. In 1917, "dazzle" camouflage was created to confuse the enemy. The combinations of wild checkerboard, striped, and swirling patterns painted on the ship made it difficult to pinpoint through a submarine periscope. As the decorated ship moved through the rough waters, the color and pattern changes proved an optical illusion. Where was the ship? How large was it? Was it really *two* ships?

British painter Edward Wadsworth's *Dazzle-Ships in drydock at Liverpool*, shows four men dwarfed by the ship they are painting. Wadsworth not only captured the job on canvas, he oversaw the painting of over two thousand dazzle ships in Britain.

CAMOUFLAGE

"Now, then, children, what's this animal?"
"Please, teacher, it's a horse wot's put on a bathing suit to deceive the Germans."

By Hilda Cowham

Humor to the rescue again. This cartoon from an English magazine demonstrates that school children knew about dazzle ships and camouflage. (Bathing suits of the period were often long-legged and striped.)

. . . And in the Air

Only two aviators and one airplane accompanied the first Canadian troops sent to England in 1914. By the end of the war, almost 22,000 men were in the Royal Flying Corps (RFC). At first, pilots flew over the fields determining the location of the enemy, making maps, and taking photographs. But it didn't take long for both sides to "up-grade" their planes into new weapons, attack machines in the air.

Armed with machine guns and bombs, German and Allied planes flew over their enemies, destroying trenches, villages, and thousands of lives.

(left) Before the war, huge dirigible (steered) airships called Zeppelins, were widely used to carry passengers, who sat in the gondola section suspended from the rigid balloon. This 1910 postcard has a moonlit vista and a three-dimensional gold-metal airship attached. The card highlights the romance of travel by air.

The Zeppelin was named for its creator, German general and aeronautical pioneer Count Ferdinand von Zeppelin, who died before the war ended. In 1915, Zeppelins carried out the first bombing raid over England, and the Allies grew to fear the sound of their approach. The airship became an image of destruction, not romance. This depiction (above) is from a children's book that entertained boys with war stories of courage and boy-heroism.

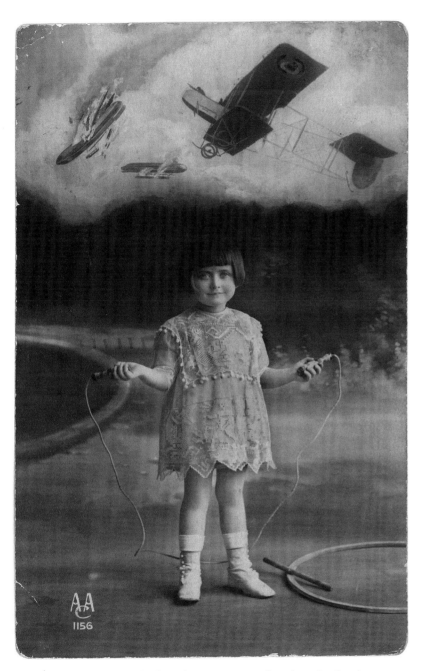

The two "Williams of the Air."
(above) William Avery (Billy) Bishop
(1894-1956) became the first Canadian
pilot to win the Victoria Cross, a medal for
acts of bravery. Bishop was credited with
destroying 72 German aircraft.
(left) William Barker (1894-1930) was also
a First World War ace. (An ace was a pilot
who had shot down five or more enemy
planes.) Barker had 53 aerial victories and
was awarded the Victoria Cross in 1918
after his single-handed combat with 60
enemy aircraft. After the war, he was the
first director of the newly-established
Royal Canadian Air Force.

(above) A little girl dressed in lace plays jump-rope. Above her a bi-plane brings two
Zeppelins down in flames. This bizarre combination of war and everyday images is a
startling reminder of the impact of the seemingly never-ending Great War.

"You Have Suffered Terribly"

At the war's outset, trained nuns or "nursing sisters" treated the wounded. But as the conflict continued, more nurses were needed. Women from all walks of life were recruited and trained to handle the massive number of casualties.

Some nurses remained in England to work in convalescent hospitals. Others were sent to France where they worked beside the doctors in field hospitals and dressing stations. They toiled in make-shift hospitals where materials were in short supply. Surgery often took place while the enemy bombarded the building.

Injured men were taught to use their "First Field Dressing" when hit. The small kit package contained a wool pad, a square piece of gauze, a bandage, and pin. The soldier was to bind his own wound — and wait on the field for further help. Later, he might be sent to a hospital to recuperate. At left, local children bring smiles to hospital patients.

(right) The wounded share a moment's fun with the medical staff. Canadian nurses were nicknamed "bluebirds" because they wore bright blue cotton uniforms for hospital duty. Some of the men are wearing their metal hats which weighed more than two and one half pounds (one kilogram).

(above) Caught in action forever on a memorial in Westmount Park, Montreal, Canada, this nurse stands beside a soldier in a wheelchair and looks toward another call for help.

Nurses were among the victims of the shelling and disease. The tremendous impact their work had on the lives of the injured earned them military decorations and a new respect for women as a significant force on the battlefields of the world.

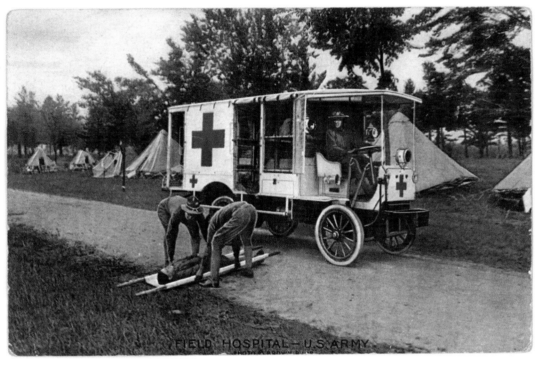

FIELD HOSPITAL — U.S. ARMY

REPAIRING A MAN OF WAR

(above) This U.S. Army ambulance is motorized and has special headlights. Some ambulances were drawn by horses. The vehicles were used to move the wounded to the rear of the field for further attention. *Note the sturdy construction throughout and the gigantic red cross on its side which secures for it immunity from attack.* The description of the ambulance also mentions that it could be a bumpy ride as the ambulance drove over the rutted roads.

' "Poor boy, you have suffered terribly." '

(above and left) The "efficient nurse" appeared in books, magazines, and artwork as a comforting figure. She is always depicted (even in photographs) as clean, pretty, hardworking, and in control amidst the chaos. At a time of limited medical equipment and drugs, and prolific rats, fleas, and lice, the nurse's presence had a calming effect. Often, it was a nurse who tended to a soldier in his dying moments — and relayed that information to his family.

Propaganda & Patriotism

During wartime, attempts to change the emotions and opinions of people were plentiful. Propaganda was information sent out to help or damage a cause. It was manufactured and distributed around the world, through posters, paintings, songs, and literature. Similar materials appealed to a family's patriotism, their love of, or loyalty to, their country and cause. Sometimes it is difficult to sort one from the other.

(below) This photo of 155 shells, called "The New Flowers of the Fields," impresses the viewer with the might of the weaponry, and perhaps the strength of the protection — or attack.

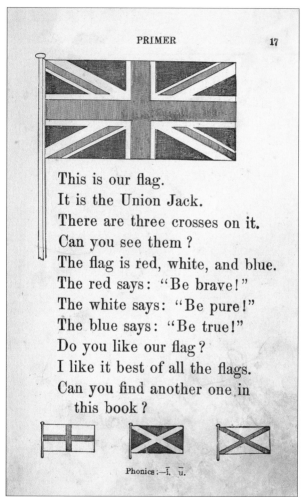

(above) A page from *The Ontario Readers Primer*, used during the Great War, impresses upon the beginning reader the importance of bravery, purity, and truth.

CAMPAGNE DE 1914-1916

Visé Paris Nº 624
Les nouvelles Fleurs des Champs. Obus de 155 dissimulés sous des branchages.
The News flowers of the fields 155 shells hidden under some boughs. ND. Phot.

Don't be Alarmed, the
Canadians
are on guard.

The flag he loves is the flag you love,
He swore its honor to defend.
One hundred million Americans
Will back him to the very end!

PROPAGANDE ALLEMANDE

— (On ne croirait pas que j'ai tué la mère.)

(above left and middle) Images of flags unfurled in the breeze, a handsome young soldier promising protection, and U.S. President Woodrow Wilson, all provoke emotional responses designed to boost morale and commitment to the war effort.

(above) *German Propaganda* is the title of this French postcard. A burly German soldier smiles and tells the photographer *"No one will believe I killed the mother,"* as he feeds the French child. How could someone see this and not despise the enemy?

(left) Likewise, hatred is provoked by this painting of a huge drunken and armed German soldier asleep in a French family's cottage. He and all he represents fill half the picture. The weeping children and their vanquished mother pull at the heart. The image is based on truth, for armies commandeered, or took over, houses for their own use.

25

![1918 War-Time Recipe Book cover]

Cooks were reminded that *In God's name, what are eggs and tea compared with final victory?* They were told *Eat more fish — save Bread, Beef and Bacon for the Armies.* During the war years, items like these were shipped to the troops overseas. After delivery, the stacked, crated rations looked like wooden mountains.

"Keep the Home Fires Burning"

So began a popular wartime song. The next lines are: *While your hearts are yearning, though your lads are far away they dream of Home.*

Home. Whether a farmhouse on the prairies or a cozy house in one of North America's big cities, it was physically far from the Front, but was tied to Europe nevertheless. Everyone's life was affected by the news that arrived via newspapers, magazines, and public announcements. Every aspect of family business and pleasure was filled with reminders. The war would only be won if *everyone* worked together. Work they did, even the children who created war gardens for food supplies.

(above) Women who hadn't taken on factory jobs during the war were at home rolling bandages, and knitting thousands of socks and wrist cuffs to keep the men warm and dry. This sculpture pays tribute to the home workers.

(left) Amateur stage shows helped raise funds because the war was expensive. (Notice the men's parts are being played by women. At the Front, men dressed as women when the troops had time for variety shows.) Vaudeville stars tickled theatre audiences with tongue-twisters like *Sister Susie's sewing shirts for soldiers*. Later in the war, the troops enjoyed stars such as Charlie Chaplin when outdoor theatres allowed them to see the same films as the folks back home.

WAR-TIME SAVINGS

Save the pennies

(left) Postcards meant for pleasant notes became yet another opportunity to remind a person to save. (Read the headline of the fellow's newspaper.) Smokers were educated about the war when they enjoyed a cigarette. A series of "Infantry Training" cards inside cigarette packages (below, front and back) brought the Infantry Training manual (see page 7) home.

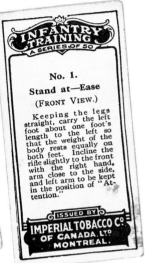

Despite the miseries of war, there was time for marriage before a soldier left, or when he was on leave. Or perhaps a verse or two of a popular song about the French city of Armentières (above before it was destroyed): *Oh, Mademoiselle from Armentières, Parlez-vous?. . . Hinky-dinky, parlez-vous?* The song had a number of optional verses, some of which could not be repeated in the company of women and children.

A Child's World

Fathers, uncles, older brothers — perhaps all had gone to war. Mothers, aunts, and older sisters were busy keeping life as normal as possible and providing for the country's wartime needs. What was it like for a young child during the war?

School, play, and chores filled their young lives, as they had before the Great War began. But school, play, and chores also changed a bit, each reflecting the war that threatened to engulf the world. A new chore would have been packing handkerchiefs, peppermint drops, and pencils in a gift box for a soldier, perhaps their father, at the Front.

(above) Barefoot out in the field, he's Mummy's little soldier — without boots! Photographs were taken of children in miniature uniforms and perhaps their family soldier's hat. Compare the boy's uniform with the spiffy version worn by the lad representing the British forces in the brightly-colored postcard (right). This is one of a popular series that featured children playing the parts of the nations at war. Here, brave Britain protects little Miss France from ominous Germany.

NOT LIKELY!

(below) This card is all that remains of a board game played by children during the First World War. The language, *Call to Attention*, is military. The flags represent the Allies.

CALL TO ATTENTION.

Place one man in play.
If all men are in play, move all
men forward one circle.

(below) Armed with paper hats and wooden swords, these boys march across the pages of an American Grade One reader. The puppy watches patiently. How peaceful the scene is when compared to the British child's book (right). It shows a youth knocked back, but not killed, by an explosion. In actual battle, such a burst would have killed many in the trench. Here, as often was the case, the boy character is an unharmed hero.

"'I was finally knocked out with the gun.'"

OUR FLAG

STICK SMOKELESS POWDER   BLACK POWDER

Shell of Famous 75.

(above) A children's book is the source of this detailed cross-section of a shell, the very same armament that was killing thousands of people across the Atlantic.

(right) Imagine the thousands of similar messages that reached children during the war:

Dear Son,
Cheer up and look
after your Mother
for dad. I love
you darling. Say
your prayers for me
every night so dad will
come back to you.
      From dad to Cyril
For my Son
Cyril. Bless you
and Good night
XXXXXXX

Did Cyril's father return?
We will never know.

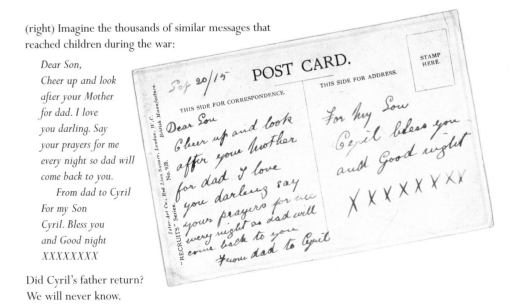

Mum's the Word

Letters and postcards were a soldier's primary link with his family while he was serving his country. Many of the letters repeated the same words: *I'm fine, don't worry about me, how's everything at home?* There wasn't too much more that a soldier could write, because if he mentioned and described where he and his comrades were, there was a chance the enemy would intercept the mail and determine the Allies' locations. "Mum's the word" (I can't tell you anything) was a phrase often repeated. For families missing a loved one, however, just the sight of his handwriting was enough consolation. Every letter received meant he was still alive.

(below) "The language of stamps" was a way to add an additional, unwritten, message to a card.

(above) Organizations such as the Young Men's Christian Association (YMCA) set up areas where soldiers would find stacks of paper, envelopes, ink bottles, and pens in order to write home. Some envelopes had a section where the soldier swore to the fact that his letter was not revealing any strategic information.

174. La Grande Guerre 1914-15-16
Aspect du Village après la bataille
Visé Paris 174 — The village's ruins A. R.

(above) The most beautiful, expensive, and popular postcards mailed by troops during the war were the "embroidered silks" from France. Pieces of silk were stiffened and colorfully stitched by French women at home, and then sent to companies who cut and enclosed the silk in an embossed paper frame.

Three examples of censored war mail:
(top left) A letter might be read by someone else before an envelope was sealed. Once the reader had determined no important information was "leaked," the envelope or postcard was marked with the red stamp "Passed Field Censor" and put into mail bags for pick-up.
(middle left) The sender has censored this card himself. He has scraped away the name of the place it shows. On the back he writes: *This is what war means to a country — just ruin.*
(bottom left) On these pre-printed cards, the soldier crossed out anything he *didn't* want to say, dated the card, and signed it. Brief and to the point — he's alive.

(above left) "Ed" sent home this elaborate French military card: *Well Mother your boy is well & happy. Things are beginning to hum. What joy. We are ready . . . Think of me now & again.*
(above right) The British soldier and flag decorate a card that brings "Hearty Greetings" for the New Year.

"The Poppy Poem"

For over eighty-five years, people have recited the war poem "In Flanders Fields," by John McCrae, a Canadian medical officer during the Great War. McCrae wrote the sonnet in May 1915, after an enemy shell exploded at the feet of his close friend, Lieutenant Alexis Helmer. Inspired by this tragedy, and the hundreds of wounded and dying men he treated routinely, the doctor wrote a poem that to this day relays the images of war, loss, love, and renewal.

McCrae sent "In Flanders Fields" to England for possible publication. It appeared, without his name, in the December 8, 1915 issue of *Punch* magazine. Later, people learned who wrote it, and the sonnet became the most popular poem of the Great War. John McCrae treated the wounded until he became ill with pneumonia in January 1918. He died within a few days and was buried with military honors in Wimereux, France.

Men were inspired by the final stanza's call-to-arms and joined the army when it most needed new recruits. In 1917 the first Victory Loan Bonds in Canada used lines from the poem in their advertisements and raised the incredible sum of 400 million dollars for the war effort.

Angels, Statues, & Songs in the Night

Throughout the war years, stories, some too incredible to believe, made their way from the Front to the rest of the world. Soldiers' letters home provided one perspective. The media, ready to latch on to anything that might keep morale high, massaged other "facts." In the end, it often didn't matter if the stories were true or not. They became part of the lore of the Great War.

The Angels of Mons

The British Expeditionary Force fought the Germans at Mons, Belgium in August 1914. Outnumbered at this first major battle of the war, the British soldiers retreated, fighting all the while. Soon after, a story about angels began to circulate. The British, it reported, had been saved by heavenly intervention — angels had appeared between the warring armies. One reference says *All the world knows the legend of the "Angels of Mons". . . On the first day of the retreat there appeared in the northern sky, like the twin forms of Gabriel and Raphael — angels of Death and Faith, two winged, gigantic figures, with hands uplifted, as if they bade the German legions hold back a space, that those who fought for Right, Civilisation, and for Justice, might have time in which to rally.*

An English short-story writer, Arthur Machen, admitted that "The Bowmen," a story of his about angels and a battle, was completely untrue, but people believed what they wanted, or needed to believe. With God on their side, the Allies could not lose the war, and their sons and daughters would come home.

(right) German soldiers display their Christmas tree in the trench. The soldier with the cane conducts the squeezebox player.

Stille Nacht

On Christmas Eve 1914, in the dark trenches, the freezing soldiers awaited the enemy's next attack across No Man's Land. But there was no shooting, only silence. Afraid to peer over the parapet, the British soldiers quietly sat and listened to the rising sound of men's voices singing.

When they dared to look across the battle-scarred landscape, the British saw the gleam of tiny lights, as the Germans lit candles on small Christmas trees in their trenches. *"Stille Nacht"* ("Silent Night") filled the air as the Germans observed the holy eve of peace.

In the desolate landscape so far from home, the soldiers of both sides called a truce. They shared wine, cigars, chocolate, and sausages. On Christmas Day, No Man's Land became a soccer pitch.

The unofficial truce lasted for days and soldiers wrote to their families about the wonderful Christmas they'd had. Sadly, with the truce over, the men returned to their trenches, and the war continued for nearly four more years.

G. Lelong, 21, Rue St-Martin, Amiens — Visé Paris n° 213

Guerre 1914-1916

111 — ALBERT (Somme) - La Place Faidherbe - Le Pensionnat de Mlle Cordier, Rue Jeannne d'Harcourt après le bombardemont. — The Place Faidherbe after the bombardment.

Our Lady of Brebières

During the Battle of the Somme in 1916, thousands of soldiers passed the Church of Notre Dame de Brebières in the town of Albert, France. At the top of the church tower was a golden figure of Mary holding the Infant Jesus up to the heavens.

The statue was knocked over, but did not fall to the ground during a shell bombardment in 1915. Albert was ruined, but Our Lady remained atop the church. The statue was secured as it was until it could be properly mended later.

A legend grew that said if the statue fell, the war would end. In the spring of 1918, the Germans captured the town and the statue fell. By the end of the year the war was over.

The church has been restored. The golden Lady of Brebières now surveys a rebuilt Albert and once again holds her baby aloft.

Spies & Traitors — Or Not?

Espionage, or spying, was a natural development of the war. Each side wanted to know what the other was planning, and the best way to find out was to send secret agents into the enemy camp. The public was warned that any stranger in their midst, or even a friend, could be listening and watching and reporting to the enemy. Men and women were captured, imprisoned, sometimes tried and executed as spies. Concrete evidence was not always available — fear brought swift "justice" to the innocent and guilty alike.

Two of the more famous "spies" of the First World War were women whose cases continue to be debated over eighty-five years later.

MATA-HARI

Mata Hari

Margaretha Geertruida Zelle was born in Holland in 1876 and lived in East Java after her marriage. In the early 1900s, unskilled and without income, she created a new persona, that of "Mata Hari" ("Eye of the Dawn" in Malay), the beautiful exotic dancer whose shimmering bangle bracelets and scanty clothing won many male admirers.

Some of Mata Hari's Allied lovers were privy to military and political information that the Germans wanted to know. She was a member of the German secret service, and the British, French, and Germans *all* suspected her activities. Today, historians believe her arrest in Paris in February 1917, was a result of the general nervousness of the time and an impulsive reaction to the defeat of the French in recent battles. After a highly-publicized trial, where her lifestyle was of great interest, Mata Hari was executed by a French firing squad in October 1917. But had she *really* been a traitor? If so, for which side had she been working?

Edith Cavell

This patriotic postcard features the serene face of English nurse Edith Cavell, who worked in German-occupied Belgium during the war. As matron of the Berkendael Medical Institute, she was able to help more than 200 British, French, and Belgian soldiers escape from the Germans through an underground network.

In August 1915, the Germans raided the home of a network member and soon after arrested Cavell. She was tricked into admitting she had given help to Allied soldiers, and after a two-day trial, she and four Belgians were sentenced to death.

(left) Despite pleas from various governments, Edith Cavell was executed by firing squad on October 12, 1915. One of her appointed executioners was shot when he refused to fire at her. He was buried near her and the other victims. (Grave #5 is Edith Cavell's)

The news of Cavell's execution swept the world. Recruitment doubled during the eight weeks after her death. The image of the enemy as a monster was stronger than ever.

(above) After the war, in 1919, Edith Cavell was re-buried in her native England. Thousands lined the streets as her funeral cortege made its way to Westminster Abbey in London for a memorial service. Her words *"Patriotism is not enough. I must have no hatred or bitterness for anyone"* are engraved on monuments in honor of this dedicated nurse who, in only one war-year, contributed so much to the Allies' efforts.

Man's Best Friend

Some of the most upsetting photographs of the First World War are those that show the unbelievable loss of animal life. When shells devastated villages, or plunged into lines of marching troops, the hard-working animals who served the forces in a variety of ways became casualties alongside the men and women they lived with.

CANADIANS EXERCISING THEIR HORSES ON SALISBURY PLAIN.

Pals !

(above) Millions of horses were needed by the troops in Europe. Here, some are exercised in England before being shipped to France. Motor vehicles, including some early-model armored cars, were in short supply. (London's famous double-decker buses were sent over and camouflaged to serve as troop carriers.)

(right) Soldiers treated their animals with a great deal of care and love. Some brought their horses from home, and the deaths of the animals brought more hardship to the soldiers.

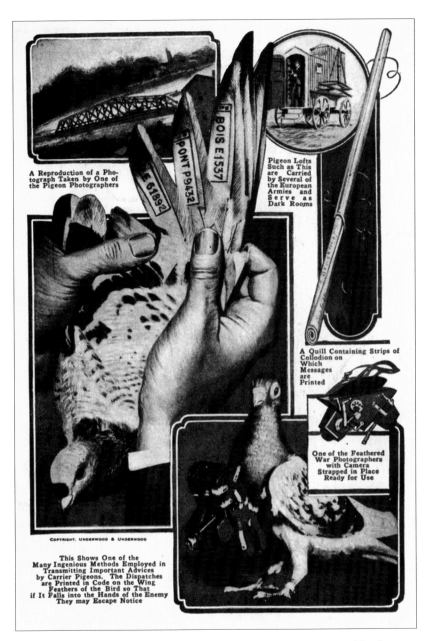

A Reproduction of a Photograph Taken by One of the Pigeon Photographers

Pigeon Lofts Such as This are Carried by Several of the European Armies and Serve as Dark Rooms

A Quill Containing Strips of Collodion on Which Messages are Printed

One of the Feathered War Photographers with Camera Strapped in Place Ready for Use

COPYRIGHT, UNDERWOOD & UNDERWOOD

This Shows One of the Many Ingenious Methods Employed in Transmitting Important Advices by Carrier Pigeons. The Dispatches are Printed in Code on the Wing Feathers of the Bird so That if It Falls into the Hands of the Enemy They may Escape Notice

Pigeons with individual names such as "Cher Ami" and "Kaiser" were used by the military to photograph the enemy troops (see small camera attached to chest), and to carry messages when other methods of communication were cut off. Often, two pigeons were sent with the same message to ensure that at least one got through to its home loft. They flew missions day and night, enduring bad weather and sprays of bullets.

CAPTURED AT COURCELETTE

As towns were destroyed and the inhabitants loaded their carts and fled, family pets were often left behind. Soldiers adopted the dogs and cats who brought them a bit of the comfort of home. ("Bonneau" was the dog befriended by John McCrae.) Unfortunately, when the troops left an area, they weren't always able to take their new friends with them.

TERRIERS.

The Germ-hun   worriers.

Dogs were trained by the military to carry messages, act as sentries, and to locate wounded men. After the war, a War Dog Memorial was built in Hartsdale, New York. A ceremony is held there every May to honor the military dogs of the Great War, and the wars that followed. Because of their appeal, animals were also used to manipulate people's emotions. One example is the card on the left.

Bear cubs, like "Bruin" here, were sometimes kept as pets or mascots at military training camps. But the most famous World War I bear was the pet of Harry Colebourn, a Canadian soldier from Winnipeg. In 1914, Colebourn left home for war. He bought an orphaned black bear cub in White River, Ontario and named him "Winnie," after his hometown. When he was shipped from England to the front, Colebourn donated Winnie to the London Zoo. It was there that young Christopher Milne saw the bear and renamed his teddy bear "Winnie the Pooh." The boy's father, A.A. Milne, went on to write the Pooh books about his son and Winnie.

SCENES IN THE CANADIAN CAMP. "BRUIN," THE PET OF THE HEADQUARTERS STAFF.

"Dear Cora..." A Soldier Doesn't Return

With his swagger stick tucked under his arm, Les posed with Cora and Helen before leaving for training camp. All the while, he sent letters and postcards to his family.

Dear Cora, Just a few lines to let you know that we arrived all safe and sound [in England] and had a very good voyage. It was pretty tough for a day and a night but there were very few sick so we couldn't kick very much at that . . . I guess I will run up to London and see the smoke and fog . . .

The story of the Lyle family is just one of the millions about families whose loved ones never returned from the war.

William Leslie Lyle was born in 1886 on Prince Edward Island, Canada. The family name had originally been DeLisle, a French name. "Les" had two brothers and a sister, Helen Leona.

Les and a brother headed west to work as decorative painters. They painted the ceilings and murals at the beautiful Pantages Theatre in downtown Toronto, and found similar work in Winnipeg. There, Les met and married Cora Wickett, and the Lyle family was soon blessed with a daughter, Helen. When Les enlisted, he became Private W.L. Lyle, #871016. (All soldiers had a "service number.") Les was sent to training camp, and then to England, and later France, where he continued to write to his family.

After Les found out how much Cora enjoyed the flower-covered silk postcards (see page 31), he sent more of them to Winnipeg. He also wrote

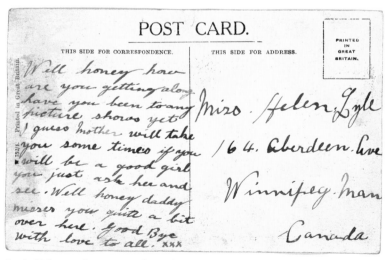

Little Helen got her own mail: *Well honey how are you getting along. Have you been to any picture shows yet. I guess Mother will take you some times if you will be a good girl. You just ask her and see. Well honey Daddy misses you quite a lot over here. Good Bye, with love to all. XXX*

letters at the YMCA and Church Army Recreation Huts. *Feb 18, 1917 Well Cora we landed in France all o.k. and there is sure some mud all right but . . . am still feeling fine . . . There isn't much news to tell you — mum is the word over here . . .*

Dec 26, 1917 We ate [our Christmas dinner] in a big tent like a circus tent, some class, eh what?

On August 31, 1918, in what appears to be his last letter to Cora, Les plays with a bit of code. Knowing the censor will read his letter, he answers a question Cora obviously asked in a previous letter — where in France are you?

Remember the title of that new song they had got up[?] Some song. Well we just finished there and we are at the same old place you were asking about.

The song may have been "Mademoiselle From Armentières" — "*some song*" with its racy words. Les is writing about that city and one nearby, Arras. Les Lyle died on September 3, 1918 fighting on the road from Arras to Cambrai, France. He was buried in nearby Wancourt. Just ten weeks later, the war was over.

(above) At some point, probably in 1918, this photograph arrived in Winnipeg. It must have disturbed Cora to see what the war had done to her husband. He looks tired and much older than his 32 years. His boots are worn and salt-stained. He has put on weight — he doesn't look well. He is with the Canadian Machine Gun Corps.

Cora was a widow at 25. For many years she wore the mourning necklace (left) with locket photographs of young Helen, and Les, *before* he left for war. She never remarried. She worked at a fruit market and soda fountain (far left) and supported her daughter, her mother, and her six brothers and sisters. Cora Lyle passed away in 1961. The Winnipeg theatre that Les Lyle decorated with murals still stands.

"Dear Amy ..." A Soldier Returns

In 1892, Frederick Rawson was born in Nottingham, England. He was the eighth and last child, and only son. His mother died when Fred was born and within three years, the Rawson children were orphans.

Fred lived with an aunt until 1907, when he sailed alone to a new life in Canada. The fifteen-year-old became a butcher's apprentice in Hamilton, Ontario. He boarded with the Edwards family and fell in love with their daughter Amy. When the war interrupted their relationship, Fred wrote to her regularly. But Fred was a victim of the gas attacks at Ypres in Spring, 1915. When he was returned home, he learned that Amy had received almost none of his letters, because her jealous father had intercepted them. Nevertheless, the couple married in late 1915.

When war broke out in 1914, sturdy Frederick Rawson enlisted. As Private Rawson, Fred trained in Quebec and on England's Salisbury Plain. Soon he was in the trenches of Flanders. Within the year, Fred Rawson was sent back home, his lungs damaged and his spirit broken.

(right, back and front) One of the few cards Amy received from Fred. *Dear Amy, I am safe and will write a letter first chance I get. God Help our 1st Contingent if this keeps up. Fondest Love, Fred x x x x x*

Like many of the soldiers who returned, Fred never said much about the war he'd experienced. (Later, his three children, Frederick, Elva, and Phyllis learned that he'd received medals for his service.) But just as Fred's days of fighting were over, so were his days of good health, for the gas had damaged his lungs and stomach. It was hard for him to keep down a meal.

During the flu epidemic of 1918, Fred Rawson was one of the millions of people around the world who contracted the illness. His weakened lungs were susceptible, and by Christmas Day, Fred was in the hospital. The man who during the war had given his daily rum rations to his comrades, found that whiskey made him feel better. Fred, like many soldiers who returned from the Great War, developed a taste for alcohol. But by the time he was 37, ill and afraid of losing his family, Fred focused on the bus company he'd set up in Belleville, Ontario instead of on drinking. He was a successful businessman providing a much-needed transport service when he died in 1934, only 42 years old.

Amy Edwards Rawson and her children carried on with her husband's bus company during the years of the Great Depression. When World War II began in 1939, the family expanded the Rawson Bus Company and drove the Royal Canadian Air Force airmen and civilian workers to the base in nearby Trenton. The company was eventually sold to the Belleville Transit Commission. Amy Rawson passed away in 1980 at the age of 93.

Private Frederick Rawson was deprived of a long, healthy life by the clouds of gas that blew across No Man's Land in 1915. But the stories of his laughter, his piano-playing, and his business enterprises have kept his spirit alive for his family's future generations.

Before the war ended, Fred started a taxi business. The Rawson family was known for the fun they had, the jokes they played on one another, and the music they made in the parlor when their relatives dropped by for a visit.

The Budding of Remembrance

There was plenty for everyone to remember when the war ended on Armistice Day — at the 11th hour of the 11th day of the 11th month, 1918. Germany was defeated. Soon soldiers would be demobilized, or disbanded, and sent home. For them, life would never be the same again. The small red flower that had dotted the scarred landscape and adorned soldiers' helmets would soon become a symbol of all that had been lost and accomplished.

Just two days before the Armistice, Miss Moina Belle Michael of Athens, Georgia decided that the Flanders poppy of John McCrae's poem should be recognized nationally as a memorial

VERSAILLES 28 Juin 1919
Signature de la Paix

(above) Reflections flicker in the Hall of Mirrors in Paris on June 28, 1919. U.S. President Woodrow Wilson, France's Premier Georges Clemenceau, and Britain's Prime Minister Lloyd George are among those about to sign the Treaty of Versailles, which will set the terms of compensation by Germany. Humiliated, the German delegates sit on the other side of the table.

(right) The signing of the peace treaty launched more celebrations. In July 1919, the departing American troops marched grandly down Parisian avenues.

LES FÊTES DE LA VICTOIRE A PARIS — 14 JUILLET 1919
Le Défilé - Troupes Américaines

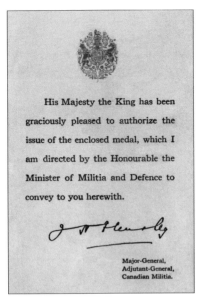

flower. By 1920, the poppy was officially adopted in the United States. A year later, silk poppies were being made by French widows and orphans and sold, with the profits going to veterans' families or programs for disabled veterans. Similar efforts continue today in many countries around the world.

"Poppy mania" continued through the 1920s and communities were urged to plant poppy gardens. The sturdy flower that decorated the hastily dug graves in Flanders, and survived the ravages of war, has come to represent our remembrance of life, sacrifice, and honor.

(above) In Canada, soldiers gradually received their medals — and began to adapt to a new life.
(below) Psychological and physical injuries made re-entry into the work force difficult or impossible.

United States Employment Service

Camp Dix, New Jersey

5/23 191 9

United States Employment Service

32? So Main St

Phillipsburg, NJ

This card is presented by Frederick L Sutle

Street City Phillipsburg State Pa

who is being released from military service and whose previous occupation was

.... EVERY EFFORT SHOULD BE MADE TO PLACE THIS MAN IN SATISFACTORY EMPLOYMENT.

Registered by Wm. R. Banks

(See other side for location of New Jersey offices.)

(above) In the United States, men who were no longer employed by the Army were issued cards to help them find "satisfactory employment."

(below) Moina Belle Michael died during the Second World War. Newspapers reported *that her grave was covered with a blanket of 3,223 red poppies which had been made by veterans.* Four years later, a U.S. stamp was issued in her honor.

In Solemn Tribute

(above) The Canadian War Memorial at St. Julien, Belgium shows a soldier at rest with his rifle reversed (bayonet towards the ground) — a symbol of peace and respect.

(below) The Cenotaph, in London, England, is not a grave stone — it represents all those who died in the war and are buried elsewhere.

Not long after the war was over, the governments of the world went about reburying the dead. Those who had been buried quickly while bombs burst above, were permanently interred in peaceful, landscaped cemeteries. Monuments were erected as cities and towns were re-built. Annual, sometimes daily, remembrance ceremonies became a part of life — proof that those who survived the Great War would not forget.

(below) A World War I cemetery before the uniform white marble stones were in place.

(above) Each day, traffic is stopped at Ypres' Menin Gate and "The Last Post" is played on the bugle in memory of those who have died in war.

In Ottawa, Canada, solid larger-than-life figures representing all parts of the forces stand at the base of the National War Memorial. In May 2000, the remains of Canada's Unknown Soldier were brought from Vimy, France to permanently rest at the foot of this memorial. He, unlike so many others, has come home at last.

Each year, thousands visit the cemeteries of Europe and pause at the graves of those known and unknown to them.

Acknowledgements

Heartfelt thanks are extended by the author to Kathryn Cole, whose dedication to the memory of our World War I veterans helped bring this book to life. Gratitude also goes to Dave Campbell, Dartmouth, Nova Scotia; Mrs. Elva Cole, Toronto; Leona Trainer, Toronto; Michael Martchenko, Toronto; Emma Cummings and Janice Mullin, The Imperial War Museum, London; The New York Times Agency, Nora Hague & Stéphanie Poisson of the McCord Museum of Canadian History, Montreal; Sherry Stewart of the National Archives of Canada, Ottawa; Sylvia Hoffmann and Margret Schulze of Ullstein Bild, Berlin; Raven Amiro of the National Gallery of Canada, Ottawa; the staff of the Toronto Reference Library; David Bennett of Transatlantic Literary Agency Inc.; and to the many friends who have listened patiently to 'war stories.' Special thanks to Blair Kerrigan, who deftly commanded the many images into marching order, and to my troops at home, Cal, Brian and Devon Smiley.

Picture Credits

Grateful acknowledgement is made to all those who have granted permission to reprint copyrighted and personal material. Every reasonable effort has been made to locate the copyright holders for these images. The publisher would be pleased to receive information that would allow them to rectify any omissions in future printings.

All illustrative materials, including cover images, are from the Author's collection except where noted.
Page 4, left: The New York Times Agency; 10, left: courtesy of Malcolm Cullen; 19, top: permission of The Trustees of the Imperial War Museum, London/Q 21493; 19, bottom left: National Gallery of Canada, Ottawa/# 8925, transfer from the Canadian War Memorials, 1921; 21, top right: Rider-Rider, William/National Archives of Canada/PA-001654; 21, bottom right: National Archives of Canada/ PA-122516; 32, left: detail, Memorial tribute to John McCrae, copied 1925, View-23398/Notman Photographic Archives, McCord Museum of Canadian History, Montreal; 32, right: National Archives of Canada/C26561; 35, top: ullstein bild/ #7.864; 40-41: courtesy of Leona Trainer and family; 42-43: courtesy of Elva Cole and family; 47: courtesy of Michael Martchenko.

Index